JOSHUA
DISOBEYS

JOSHUA DISOBEYS

Written and Illustrated by

Dennis Vollmer

LANDMARK EDITIONS, INC.

P.O. Box 4469   •   1402 Kansas Avenue   •   Kansas City, Missouri 64127

(816) 241-4919

Dedicated to

my brother, Daniel,
and to all other children who have
cerebral palsy and brain injury.

Fourth Printing

COPYRIGHT©1988 BY DENNIS VOLLMER

International Standard Book Number: 0-933849-12-5 (LIB.BDG.)

Library of Congress Cataloging-in-Publication Data
Vollmer, Dennis, 1980-
   Joshua disobeys.
   Summary: When Joshua, a baby whale, disobeys his mother and swims too close to
shore to visit with a friendly human boy, he becomes stranded on the beach. Includes
factual information about whales in a separate section in the back of the book.
   [1. Whales — Fiction.   2. Obedience — Fiction.]

I. Title.
PZ7.V8874Jo   1988   [E]   88-9464

Editorial Coordinator: Nancy R. Thatch
Creative Coordinator: David Melton
Production Assistant: Dav Pilkey

Landmark Editions, Inc.
P.O. Box 4469
1402 Kansas Avenue
Kansas City, Missouri 64127
(816) 241-4919

Printed in the United States of America

JOSHUA DISOBEYS

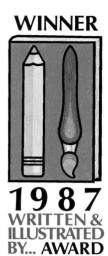

When we initiated THE NATIONAL WRITTEN & ILLUSTRATED BY... AWARDS CONTEST FOR STUDENTS in 1986, teachers throughout the nation loved the idea. Most of them thought the CONTEST was wonderful for top-ranking students, but some felt less academically skilled students would not be able to compete. Still others doubted younger students would stand a chance of winning.

However, six-year-old Dennis, a Chapter I student who was about to repeat the first grade, didn't know he wasn't supposed to be able to compete. So he wrote and illustrated JOSHUA DISOBEYS and entered it in the 1987 CONTEST. Competing with more than 3,600 entries from all 50 states in the Union, his book was declared the WINNER in the 6 to 9 age category.

JOSHUA DISOBEYS is a book of exceptional skill and imagination. Dennis's exciting and thoughtful story is simple, but effectively told. Its structure is complete with a good sense of a beginning, middle and end. The setting is introduced and characters are developed in the course of the plot.

Dennis's illustrations are extraordinary displays of creative genius. Anyone who is familiar with the paintings of six-year-old children will surely recognize that Dennis's use of overlaying colors is quite accelerated for one so young.

Viewers should be fascinated to see elements of van Gogh, Matisse, Chagall and Seurat within Dennis's work. I doubt that young Dennis has studied the works of these great artists. But I have a feeling when he sees their paintings, he will probably conclude, "Hey, those guys paint just like I do." I also suspect if Messrs. van Gogh, Matisse, Chagall and Seurat could see Dennis's illustrations, they would consider such a comparison to be a compliment.

NOTE — As Dennis's book was about to go to press, his grandmother, Arlene Hanley, phoned to tell us some extraordinary news. At the beginning of the 1987 school year, Dennis's reading skill test score was in the 15th National Percentile, but by year's end, his score ranked in the 97th National Percentile. Ms. Hanley is convinced Dennis's experience in creating an original book was a major factor in improving his academic skills. She also believes winning the CONTEST was a tremendous plus toward increasing his self-esteem.

While Landmark is thrilled with Dennis's achievement and pleased to think we contributed to his success, we know we were only one element in the concerted efforts of Dennis's supportive family, caring teachers, and dedicated grandmother. We wish all children's lives could be affected in such positive ways.

So now, sit back, turn the pages, read Dennis's wonderful story about a baby whale, and enjoy his amazing illustrations.

Only six years old? Yes, he is!

—David Melton
Creative Coordinator
Landmark Editions, Inc.

Joshua was a baby whale.
He lived in the ocean with his mother.

Joshua was big, but his mother was bigger. And some whales were even bigger than Joshua's mother.

The whales liked living in the ocean.

Joshua liked to swim in the ocean too, but he was a very curious little whale. He wondered what it would be like to live

on the land.

"No! No! No!" Joshua's mother warned. "You must never
go close to the shore. It is too dangerous!"

But one day, when Joshua's mother was not looking, he
wandered away. He swam toward the shore just to look around.
He saw sand on the beach and grass on the hills. And he saw
tall trees and beautiful flowers.

Then Joshua saw the most wonderful thing of all. He saw
a boy walking along the shore.

The boy waved his hand and called, "Hi, baby whale!"

Joshua could not stop himself — he swam a little closer.

The boy called again, this time even louder.

Joshua tried to talk through his blowholes, but only a fountain of mist spurted out.

"Come closer!" the boy yelled.

"My mother won't let me," Joshua tried to say.

"Please come closer," the boy begged.

Although Joshua knew he should not swim any closer to the shore, he did.

"My name is B.J.," the boy called. "What is your name?"

The baby whale tried to say, "Joshua," but he could not make the sounds in the boy's language.

Then Joshua swam even closer. Soon he was in shallow

water, and the sand tickled his stomach.

Then suddenly a big wave came up and pushed Joshua onto the beach. But when the water washed back into the ocean, it did not take Joshua with it.

Poor Joshua was *beached!* He could not move forward and
he could not crawl back into the water. He was stuck!

"Help!" cried the baby whale.

He hoped his mother would come and pull him back into the water. But his mother could not hear him. She was too far away.

"I'll help you!" B.J. said, and he started scooping sand away so Joshua could slide back into the water. But the baby whale was too heavy. He sank deeper and deeper into the sand.

18

So B.J. ran to get help. Many people came back with him. Some of the people dug away the sand. Others poured water on Joshua so the baby whale would not get too dry and die.

Suddenly the people heard a shrill sound. When they looked toward the ocean, they saw Joshua's mother. She was heading straight for the shore.

The people could not understand the mother whale's strange sounds, but they knew she must be scolding Joshua because he had disobeyed her.

Then an enormous wave crashed onto the beach, and Joshua's mother came with it!

All of the people were frightened. They screamed and ran for their lives.

The wave was so big that it covered all of the beach. But when the water washed back from the shore, Joshua and his mother were gone.

B.J. stood on the beach for a long time. He looked at the big ocean, but he could not see Joshua or his mother anywhere.

Finally, way out in the ocean, a big spout of mist shot up

into the air. Then a little spout shot up beside it.

B.J. knew Joshua and his mother were together again. That made B.J. happy. But he was also sad because he could not see his new friend.

B.J. wondered if he would ever see Joshua again. Maybe not.

But a few days later, when B.J. was playing on the beach, he heard the squeaking sounds of a baby whale. And believe it or not — there was Joshua!

B.J. could not hear any words in the squeaky sounds, but he knew the baby whale was trying to say, "Hi, B.J."

So B.J. waved and called back, "Hi, Joshua!"

B.J. knew Joshua understood, because the baby whale leaped up and flipped his tail back and forth.

But, this time, Joshua did not swim near the shore. He had learned his lesson.

And although B.J. and Joshua could not live in the same place, they knew they could still be friends.

Interesting Facts About Whales

Compiled by Dennis Vollmer

Whales are mammals. They are not fish. Fish breathe air through gills. Whales cannot breathe under water. They have lungs and must hold their breath like people do.

Whales are warm-blooded animals. This means their blood stays the same temperature, no matter how cold or hot the water around them may become. They also have a layer of fat, called *blubber,* which keeps them warm, just as our clothing protects us.

Fish lay eggs, but whales are born live. Like land mammals, mother whales nurse their young with milk.

Whales are divided into two main groups — **Baleen Whales** and **Toothed Whales:**

> **Baleen Whales** have baleen instead of teeth. Baleen is a sort of strainer, made of a substance like fingernails. It catches little fish, shrimp and plants for the whales to eat.

> **Toothed Whales** have peglike teeth that help them to get hold of slippery fish or squid to eat.

Whales have been on our planet for 45 million years. They are the largest animals that have ever lived on the earth or in our oceans. Some are even larger than any of the dinosaurs.

Newborn baby whales may weigh more than two large elephants.

The blue whale is the largest. It can weigh as much as 196 tons and be 100 feet long, which is about the size of a jet airliner that can seat 100 passengers.

Despite their great weight, whales can leap completely out of the water.

Whales have blowholes on top of their heads or on the tips of their snouts. These blowholes are really nostrils that whales use when breathing.

Whales can dive straight down into the ocean as deep as 2,000 feet. They can stay under water for 25 minutes or longer.

Before a whale dives, it fills its lungs with air, closes its blowholes tightly, and holds its breath. While it's under the water, the air in its lungs heats up a lot. When the whale comes back to the surface, it suddenly "blows" through its blowholes to let out the hot air. When the warm air hits the cold water, we see a fountain of mist. The same thing happens when our warm breath hits the air on a cold morning. Whales can "blow" very high. Their spouts of mist can reach as high as 50 feet into the air.

A group of whales that lives together is called a *pod.*

Whales communicate with each other. They actually learn to duplicate sounds made by other whales, just like people learn new words from other human beings.

There is a special bay in Canada, named Robson Bight, and also called the "rubbing beach," where killer whales from all over go to roll around and scratch their bellies on the beach. While they are "beach rubbing," they make noises that they don't make anywhere else in the world.

Whales are very smart. They have been trained to perform tricks at water shows. In fact, killer whales are so smart, they have been known to make up their own tricks.

Sources of Information:

Great Whales, The, National Geographic Video Documentary.
I Can Read About Whales & Dolphins, by J.I. Anderson, Troll Associates.
Killer Whales, Survival Anglia, Ltd., Video Documentary.
Mammals of the Deep, Jacques Yves Cousteau Video Documentary.
World Book Encyclopedia, The, Field Enterprises Educational Corporation.

THE NATIONAL WRITTEN & ILLUSTRATEI

— THE 1989 NATIONAL AWARD WINNING BOOKS —

Lauren Peters
age 7

Michael Cain
age 11

Amity Gaige
age 16

Dennis Vollmer
age 6

Lisa Gross
age 12

—THE 1987 NATIONAL AWARD WINNING BOOKS—

—THE 1989 GOLD AWARD WINNERS—

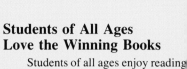

Students' Winning Books Motivate and Inspire

Each year it is Landmark's pleasure to publish the winning books of The National Written & Illustrated By... Awards Contest For Students. These are important books because they supply such positive motivation and inspiration for other talented students to write and illustrate books too!

Students of All Ages Love the Winning Books

Students of all ages enjoy reading these fascinating books created by our young author/illustrators. When students see the beautiful books, printed in full color and handsomely bound in hardback covers, they, too, will become excited about writing and illustrating books and eager to enter them in the Contest.

Enter Your Book In the Next Contest

If you are 6 to 19 years of age you may enter the Contest too. Perhaps your book may be one of the next winners and you will become a published author and illustrator too.

Stacy Chbosky
age 14

Adam Moore
age 9

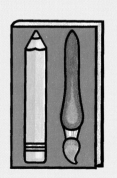

Michael Aushenker
age 19

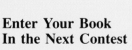

— THE 1988 NATIONAL AWARD WINNING BOOKS —

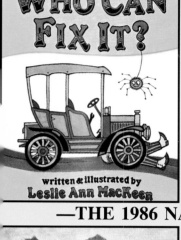

Leslie Ann MacKeen
age 9

—THE 1986 NATIONAL AWARD WINNING BOOKS—

Elizabeth Haidle
age 13

Heidi Salter
age 19

— THE 1985 GOLD AWARD WINNERS —

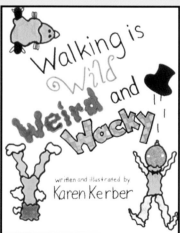

Amy Hagstrom
age 9

inners Receive Contracts, oyalties and Scholarships

The National Written & Illus-
ted by... Contest Is an Annual Event!
ere is no entry fee! The winners
eive publishing contracts, royal-
s on the sale of their books, and
-expense-paid trips to our offices
Kansas City, Missouri, where pro-
sional editors and art directors
ist them in preparing their final
nuscripts and illustrations for
blication.

Winning Students Receive
holarships Too! The R.D. and Joan
le Hubbard Foundation will award
otal of $30,000 in scholarship cer-
cates to the winners and the four
ners-up in all three age categories.
ch winner receives a $5,000 schol-
hip; those in Second Place are
arded a $2,000 scholarship; and
se in Third, Fourth, and Fifth Places
eive a $1,000 scholarship.

Isaac Whitlatch
age 11

To obtain Contest Rules, send
elf-addressed, stamped, business-
e envelope to: THE NATIONAL
RITTEN & ILLUSTRATED BY...
VARDS CONTEST FOR STU-
NTS, Landmark Editions, Inc.,
. Box 4469, Kansas City, MO
27.

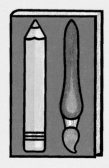

Karen Kerber
age 12

David McAdoo
age 14

Dav Pilkey
age 19

THE WRITTEN & ILLUSTRATED BY... CONTEST
— THE 1990 NATIONAL AWARD WINNING BOOKS —

Aruna Chandrasekhar
age 9

Anika Thomas
age 13

Cara Reichel
age 15

Jonathan Kahn
age 9

Jayna Miller
age 19

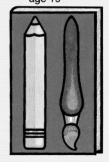

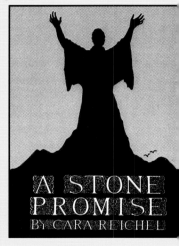

— THE 1990 GOLD AWARD WINNERS —

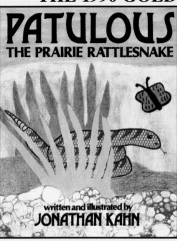

Winning the Gold Award and having my book published are two of the most exciting things that have ever happened to me. If you are a student between 6 and 19 years of age, and you li to write and draw, then create a book of your own and enter it in the Contest. Who knows? Maybe your book will be one o the next winners, and you will become a published author and illustrator too.

— Jayna Miller
Author and Illustrator
TOO MUCH TRICK OR TRE,